Buffalo Bill

Frontier Daredevil

Illustrated by E. Joseph Dreany

Buffalo Bill

Frontier Daredevil

by Augusta Stevenson

Aladdin Paperbacks

Aladdin Paperbacks
An imprint of Simon & Schuster
Children's Publishing Division
1230 Avenue of the Americas
New York, NY 10020
Copyright © 1948, 1959 by the Bobbs-Merrill Company, Inc.
All rights reserved including the right of reproduction
in whole or in part in any form.
First Aladdin Paperbacks edition, 1991

Printed in the United States of America

15   14   13   12

Library of Congress Cataloging-in-Publication Data
Stevenson, Augusta.
    [Buffalo Bill, boy of the plains]
    Buffalo Bill, frontier daredevil / by Augusta Stevenson;
illustrated by E. Joseph Dreany. —1st Aladdin Books ed.
        p.   cm. — (The Childhood of famous Americans series)
    Reprint. Originally published: Buffalo Bill, boy of the plains.
Indianapolis: Bobbs-Merrill, [1959].
    Summary: Concentrates on the boyhood of Bill Cody, Pony Express
rider, scout, showman, and buffalo hunter.
    ISBN 0-689-71479-3
    1. Buffalo Bill, 1846–1917—Childhood and youth—Juvenile
literature.   2. Pioneers—West (U.S.)—Biography—Juvenile
literature.   3. Frontier and pioneer life—West (U.S.)—Juvenile
literature.   4. West (U.S.)—Biography—Juvenile literature.
[1. Buffalo Bill, 1846–1917—Childhood and youth.   2. West (U.S.)—
Biography.]   I. Dreany, E. Joseph, ill.   II. Title.   III. Title:
Buffalo Bill, frontier dare devil.   IV. Series.
F594.B94S74   1991   978'.02'092—dc20   [B]   [92]   90-23787   CIP
                                                            AC

*To Elsie Stokes, whose interest
in my books of this series has been a source
of great encouragement to me*

Illustrations

Full pages

Numerous smaller illustrations

Contents

Books by Augusta Stevenson

ABRAHAM LINCOLN: The Great Emancipator
BENJAMIN FRANKLIN: Young Printer
BUFFALO BILL: Frontier Daredevil
CLARA BARTON: Founder of the American Red Cross
DANIEL BOONE: Young Hunter and Trapper
GEORGE WASHINGTON: Young Leader
MOLLY PITCHER: Young Patriot
NATHAN HALE: Boston Patriot
WILBUR AND ORVILLE WRIGHT: Young Fliers

★ ★ Buffalo Bill

Frontier Daredevil

Trade with the Kickapoos

THE INDIAN trader, Isaac Cody, stopped his ox team in a little clearing at the foot of a steep hill.

"Well, this is Salt Creek Valley," he said to the handsome boy on the seat beside him.

"Look, Pa! There are hills all the way around it."

"I told you it was the prettiest valley I had ever seen." Then Isaac jumped down to the ground, and his eight-year-old son followed him.

"Some campers made this clearing in just the right place for us, Bill. It's close to the trail, and that's where we have to be for trade."

"Look how wide the trail is!"

"That shows it is traveled by many feet."

"Indian feet?"

"Of course. There's a large Kickapoo village a few miles away."

While they talked, Bill helped to lift the heavy yoke from the tired oxen. He was very strong for his age. He knew how to do things, too, and he did them without being told.

He took the oxen to the creek and watered them. He tethered them in a grassy place so they could graze. Then he went back to the wagon. There was plenty to do to get ready for customers.

Mr. Cody had pushed the heavy white cover to the front and had let down the endgate. Now Bill helped him unpack the merchandise.

They were alone in this Kansas wilderness. There wasn't a white person nearer than Fort Leavenworth, six miles away. But Bill didn't think about this. He was born on the frontier in Iowa in February 1846, and, until a month ago, had lived there all his life.

The Cody family had then moved to Weston, Missouri, a town on the Missouri River. It was about four miles above Fort Leavenworth which was on the Kansas side of the river. It was five miles above the town of Leavenworth, Kansas, also on the Missouri River.

The father and son worked for some time without talking. They were too busy to say anything. The merchandise had to be arranged before any Indian customers came. Finally, Mr. Cody broke the silence.

"Yes, this valley is in a splendid place for trade. This trail goes on to the Far West, all the way to California. It's the one the gold seekers use. And there are hundreds of families moving out to Oregon now. We'll see their big covered wagons passing along."

"Won't they buy our things?"

"We can't count on them. They have to travel light. And they are all poor people looking for a better place to live. I want the Indian trade. It will be steady, year in and year out. I can come back with other loads. I might even build a log storehouse and stay here."

"Stay? You mean live here? All of us?"

There was fright in the boy's voice, and Mr. Cody noticed it. But he only smiled and said it would be a beautiful place for all of them.

"This land belongs to the Indians," he went on. "But if I can get the good will of the Kickapoo chief, I'll have no trouble about living here. The question is, how to get his good will. Shall I go to his village, or shall I wait till he comes here to trade?"

Bill didn't seem to be paying much attention to his father's words. He had taken a gun from the driver's seat and had carried it around the wagon.

14

"Pa," he said anxiously, "don't you want your gun at the back of the wagon where it will be handy?"

"Handy for what?"

"Indians."

"But, Bill, I told you this tribe here in Kansas is friendly with white people. I won't need my gun."

"Pa, I have something to tell you! A man in Weston said the Indians would kill both of us."

"That's ridiculous! Your Uncle Elijah has lived in Weston for years. He said these Kickapoos were peaceful. You know how many of them trade at his store."

"The man said they had to act that way in Missouri, because there were so many white people who lived there. But he said you couldn't trust the Kickapoos out here in this valley. He said they would scalp us."

"He was just trying to scare you, Bill. Who was he?"

"I don't know."

"Was he tall and thin? Was he round-shouldered? Was his hair coal-black?"

16

"Yes—yes." The boy nodded.

"I thought so! It was Abel Smith. He told you those things to keep me from coming here. He thought if he scared you, your mother wouldn't let you come. And she wouldn't consent to my plans, either."

"I didn't tell her."

"That's where you fooled him. Now I'll tell you a secret, Bill. This Abel Smith wanted to bring a trade wagon here himself. He tried to borrow the money in Weston, but no one would loan him a cent."

"You thought of it first, didn't you, Pa?"

Mr. Cody nodded. "Before we left Iowa. Brother Elijah wrote me about this valley. He said it would be a good place for Indian trade. He urged me to come west. He was sure I would make more money trading than I could farming."

Bill was silent for a moment. Then he burst

out, "Pa, that man made it all up about our being killed!"

"Of course. I'd rather trust the Kickapoos than Smith and his crowd. Why didn't you tell me about this right away?"

"I knew you would come anyway. And I was afraid you wouldn't bring me if you knew I was scared. I want to go everywhere you go, Pa."

Isaac patted his son's head affectionately. "Now then, you're not afraid of Kickapoos anymore, are you?"

"Not now. Do they have good ponies?"

"I think so. These prairie Indians are fine horsemen."

"Maybe you could buy a pony for me."

"I wish I could, son, but I've put all my money into this wagon and merchandise. I might be able to trade for one."

"Oh, Pa, could you?"

Mr. Cody smiled. "Well, I don't know if I

should. You might be afraid to ride a Kickapoo pony."

Bill laughed. "Abel Smith can't scare me off a pony."

"Good. We'll see what happens. Maybe some Indian customer will bring one to trade in. Now put that pile of red wool blankets here by the endgate, in plain sight. They'll go first, or I'll miss my guess."

BARGAINS FOR SQUAWS

That afternoon four squaws gazed into the back of the trade wagon and smiled and nodded.

"Pretty," said one.

Beads and brass jewelry sparkled in the sunlight. Red and green ribbons fluttered from ropes overhead. Bright-colored shawls swung from the framework were used for the cover.

Back of the endgate was a bolt of calico gleaming with red roses. Close by, the pile of

19

red wool blankets glowed warmly. Blades of long hunting knives and scissors shone like silver. Even the black cooking kettles were glossy.

The squaws pointed to this and that, and the trader told them the price. This was worth so many marten skins. This was worth so many otter skins. A saddle would take so many beaver skins. A bridle would take so many fox furs.

"Not too many skins," said the oldest squaw.

Another nodded. "Good bargain."

"We'll tell our tribe that you don't cheat," said another.

"We'll tell Chief Black Wolf," added the fourth.

They brought their bundles of furs from their ponies and began to buy. Beads, scissors, ribbons, calico, and shawls were traded for marten, otter, and fox skins. But no one bought the blankets.

The women felt them and seemed pleased. But not a skin was offered.

"Do I charge too many skins?" asked the trader.

"No! No!" the squaws cried. But still they didn't buy.

Now three women bought cooking kettles. The fourth wanted one, but there were no more. She was so disappointed she began to weep.

The others said it was too bad, and they were sorry. But no one offered to give up her kettle. "We saw them first," they said in Kickapoo language.

"Just like white women," Mr. Cody whispered to Bill, while the squaw wept louder and louder.

Then Bill remembered something. There was a frying pan with a long handle in a dark corner up front. He got it out and offered it to the weeping squaw.

She looked, grabbed it quickly and laughed aloud. "Hi! Hi! It won't burn face! I like it."

The oldest one came back. "I forgot to tell you, Trader—Chief Black Wolf will take the blankets. He's coming soon. You keep. You won't sell them to other braves?"

Mr. Cody promised.

"You won't sell them to other squaws?"

Mr. Cody promised this.

"You won't sell them to white men?"

Mr. Cody promised this also.

The squaw was pleased. "Our chief will be a friend to you—a good friend—you'll see. Good-by!"

"Good-by!" called the others, as they rode away smiling.

The squaw was pleased. "Chief be friend you—good friend—you see. Goodee-by!"

"Goodee-by!" called the others, as they rode away smiling.

Mr. Cody and Bill waved to them and then sat down on a log to talk things over.

"This is luck, Bill, just pure luck. I wanted to get the good will of this chief, but I didn't know how. Now see what happened. Four red blankets did the trick."

"Mother will laugh about it."

"Now I can bring another load. Maybe I can put up a store and start a regular trading post."

"Like Uncle Elijah's?"

"Yes indeed. Then I'll build a log cabin, and we'll move here."

"And I can have a pony."

"I hope so, Bill. Things certainly look rosy for us now."

The Red Blankets

THERE WERE no more customers that afternoon. After supper the wagon cover was stretched over the back and tied down tightly.

"The squirrels must be kept out—the crows, too," said Mr. Cody. "We don't want them stealing our jewelry."

Bill smiled at this. But he stopped smiling when he saw his father spreading their blankets under the wagon.

"We must stay close to our load," he explained. "But I'll keep a fire burning all night."

"I'll take my turn at watching the fire, if you'll wake me."

Mr. Cody laughed. "Might as well do it my-self, son. You'll have to get up early and keep camp while I go hunting. There's only enough food for our supper and breakfast."

"What if the chief comes?"

"I'll be back long before Black Wolf can get here."

Sleeping on the ground didn't bother Bill. He had done that every night on the long jour-ney from Iowa to Weston, Missouri.

But he was a little frightened when his father put his gun under the wagon within reach. "I thought fire would keep wild animals away," he said.

"It will. I may need my gun to scare away another kind of animal—gold seekers bound for California."

"Oh!"

"Some of them are all right. Others are the wrong kind. They would steal everything in the wagon. But don't worry about that, Bill. Those travelers don't start out early. They couldn't find the trail in the dark."

The traders went to sleep quickly. When Bill woke up it was broad daylight. His father was gone, and the fire was out. But he knew what to do.

First, he washed at the creek and combed his hair. Then he made a small fire. Presently the last of the corn-meal mush was frying. And then breakfast was ready, and eaten and enjoyed.

Bill knew how to clean up camp, too. The fire was put out—not a single spark was left. The frying pan was cleaned with leaves. Blankets were folded and put under the driver's seat.

As he jumped down Bill saw two white men coming along the trail. They were rough-looking, but he had seen others just as rough.

"Where are your folks, boy? Are they still asleep?" asked one.

He motioned to the wagon and Bill laughed. "There's no one in there. It's a trade wagon."

"Where's the trader?" asked the other man sharply. "And you'd better tell the truth. If you don't——" He stopped to put his hand on the pistol in his belt. "I guess you know what I mean."

"He's out hunting."

"Been gone long?"

"I don't know. I was asleep when he left."

"Stand where you are and don't move. Don't make any noise either."

The men pushed the cover back. They discovered the blankets and took them out of the wagon.

"You can't have them!" Bill cried. "They were promised to an Indian chief."

"Now isn't that too bad!" mocked one. "Sorry, boy, but these blankets will never see the inside of a tepee. They'll be traveling to California."

As the men started away, one came close to Bill and spoke threateningly. "Just one yell out of you, and it will be your last. Understand?"

"Yes, sir."

The frightened boy saw the thieves cross the brook and disappear in the brush. He knew now what they were—gold seekers—the wrong kind.

Oh, if his father would only come! He was afraid.

Suddenly he had an idea. He hurried to the brook and looked at the wet sand. Sure enough! Their footprints showed plainly. He got down on his knees and studied the marks a long time.

At last he stood. "I'd know those prints anywhere," he said to himself. "I can help Pa track them. He'll make those gold seekers give up the blankets."

BILL RIDES WITH BRAVES

It was a half hour later. The oxen had been watered and hobbled in fresh pasture. Wood had been gathered for the fire—a big pile. And still Mr. Cody hadn't come.

Now Bill heard voices and laughter. Coming along the trail were three young braves riding bareback.

"Hello!" they called gaily. "Hello!"

They reached the wagon and stopped.

"Are you the trader's boy?" asked one, smiling at Bill.

"Yes, sir."

"You're a handsome boy," said another. "Tall like an Indian."

"Brown hair—brown eyes. A very good-looking boy," declared the third.

"You are handsome, too, all of you," said Bill.

The young men laughed gaily. Then the leader said that he had come for the four red wool blankets. Chief Black Wolf couldn't come. He would send skins for pay.

Bill told them about the two gold seekers. The braves listened quietly, then talked together for a moment. The leader then turned to Bill. "We'll get the blankets. You come along—ride in front of me."

"I can't leave the wagon while Father is away."

31

"But you must come. There are lots of white men on the trail. Only you can tell us which ones robbed you. Come on!"

The boy was afraid to refuse. The brave helped him mount, and presently he was holding the horse's mane as they galloped over the prairie.

Suddenly they stopped and pointed to smoke rising from the other side of a creek. They dismounted, tied their horses and walked down the bank.

"Maybe these are not the right men," the leader whispered to Bill. "There are many campfires along this trail."

"Look!" whispered the boy. He pointed to fresh footprints in the wet sand. "Those prints match the ones I found near our wagon!"

The braves and Bill crossed the creek single file on a log. They crept up the opposite bank. Thick bushes on the top hid them completely. Now the leader peeped through a bush. Then he motioned for Bill to look.

There were the men getting breakfast! The red blankets were on a log with their guns and pistols.

Bill turned to the leader and nodded. The braves gave a war whoop and crashed through the bushes. They yelled savagely as they surrounded the two men. The gold seekers were helpless. They held up their hands. Bill was afraid they would be scalped.

One brave seized the blankets. The other seized the guns and threw them down the bank. And all the time they whooped and yelled and made frightful faces at the frightened white men.

Suddenly the Indians left. They ran down the bank, across the log and up the other bank to their ponies. They mounted. Bill rode with the leader as before.

They didn't ride fast now. They were too busy laughing and talking.

"What a joke," the leader told Bill. "We almost scared 'em to death just by making faces. That was fun!"

They reached the valley and the trade wagon. Bill jumped down, and the young braves rode away with the blankets.

Mr. Cody hadn't come, but what good news Bill had for him! The chief would get his blankets after all.

Just now he had to chase four squirrels out of the wagon. It was a good thing he hadn't been gone long. As it was, a box of beads had been turned over and Bill had a time picking them up.

"ANYTHING HAPPEN, BILL?"

A little later Mr. Cody came with game. He had three rabbits and a woodchuck—that was all. "I couldn't find much. I had to go a long

34

distance to get this. There are too many travelers passing through the valley. A good many camp here. They've scared the game away."

"I'm glad you're back, Pa. I'm awfully glad."

"Why, did anything happen?"

Bill told him. Then it was Isaac Cody's turn to be frightened. "Bill," he said, "I'll never leave you here alone again. You'll hunt with me the next time."

"And leave the wagon alone?"

"Yes. I'd rather lose everything in it than have you threatened and frightened."

Just then Bill saw two Indians coming up the trail.

"Customers, Pa! Two Indians!"

The woman was the squaw who had cried over the kettles yesterday. The other was a fine-looking warrior who sat on his horse like a king.

"Here's my father," said the squaw. "He's Chief Black Wolf, and he has come for the blankets."

The chief smiled and said he could pay with fine otter skins. They were in a bundle slung over the horse's back behind the chief.

"But the blankets are not here," said Mr. Cody. "Three of your braves came after them."

"No my braves—no send braves."

"Then who came?"

"No my braves," the chief repeated.

Mr. Cody told the whole story, and the chief listened closely. But he was suspicious. Was this trader telling the truth? He had been deceived many times by traders.

"I am sorry," said Mr. Cody, "but they told my son you had sent them."

The chief now gazed at Bill so intently the boy was embarrassed and looked down. Then he noticed something. "Look!" he cried to his father. He pointed to the chief's foot. "His moccasins are different!"

"What were the brave's moccasins like?" asked the chief quickly.

"There was a large cross made of white beads."

"Where?"

"Over the instep."

"That tribe lives far to the east. Three of their braves wanted to hunt here, but I said no. They didn't like that so they played a trick on me."

"How would they know?" asked Isaac. "No one was here after the squaws left yesterday."

"Ku!" exclaimed Black Wolf. "Women talk too much. They probably saw the hunters and told them you were here. Maybe they showed their bargains."

His daughter hung her head. That was it.

"I am sorry——" Mr. Cody began.

Chief Black Wolf made an angry gesture and turned his horse. Then he rode away. His daughter followed. And this time there were no smiles and no good-bys.

"This is bad, Bill. He thinks I didn't keep my word. He thinks I sold the blankets."

"Won't his tribe trade with us?"

"I'm afraid not."

"That's bad, Pa. We might not sell our load."

"Never mind, son. Perhaps we can find another place. Now what do you say to a nice young rabbit for dinner?"

The Singing
Trappers

THE FOLLOWING day a long train of big covered
wagons stopped in the valley. They belonged
to settlers, bound for new homes in faraway
Oregon. They were delighted to find a trade
wagon.

The children bought moccasins and Indian
dolls. The young ladies bought ribbons, beads,
and jewelry. The mothers took all the calico
and shawls. The fathers took all the hunting
knives, saddles, and bridles.

Late that afternoon Mr. Cody and Bill sat by
their campfire and talked. They had eaten an
early supper. They would go to bed early and

get an early start in the morning. They were going home to Weston. They had sold everything in the wagon.

"Ma will be glad we made so much money," said Bill.

"She will be sorry we can't move here."

Just then singing was heard in the distance. Bill was so excited he jumped to his feet. "Who is it, Pa? Indians?"

"Wait till we hear them again."

They waited a few minutes, till the music was nearer and louder. Then Mr. Cody jumped to his feet. He was excited also.

"It's trappers!" he cried. "They are coming down from the mountains. That's the 'Song of the Trappers' they are singing."

A long line of men, horses, and pack mules now came over the hilltop and began the descent to the valley.

They came slowly, singing:

The trappers come down from high mountains.
The trappers come down from cold lakes.
Real courage it took them to get there,
But they've got the courage it takes.

Their beaver is worth a small fortune.
Their otter is worth even more.
But whatever they bring,
You can count on one thing—
They'll get all the money it makes,
For they've got the courage it takes.

They stopped singing when they reached the valley and began at once to make camp.

"Oh, I hope they will sing again!" exclaimed Bill. "That was beautiful."

"They probably will, around their campfire tonight. But they have work to do now. Their animals will be taken care of before they even think of supper."

"I'm glad they camped near us. Maybe I can see them from the wagon seat. I can!" he called a minute later. "I can see everything they do."

Bill saw saddles and packs removed from tired animals. He saw them watered and fed and brushed. Then men brought wood, and fires were lighted.

Presently delicious odors drifted to the Cody camp. Bill had never, in all his life, smelled anything so wonderful. It made him hungry.

"Can't we go over there, Pa? I've never seen a trappers' camp. I'd like to know what they are cooking."

"We'll have to go right now. The trappers will post guards the minute it gets dark."

"Are they afraid of Indians?"

"No, their furs are valuable. They are taking them to a trading post to sell—probably to Leavenworth. They can't afford to have them stolen."

"They worked hard to get the beaver skins, didn't they?"

"They worked hard to get every skin in their

packs. It's a very dangerous business, Bill. Now we'll clean up a bit, and then we'll go."

TRAPPERS AND DOUGH STICKS

A little later the trappers were making Mr. Cody and his son feel at home. They were all young men, strong and hardy. They were bright and lively, too. They didn't know Mr. Cody, but they welcomed him as an old friend.

"You must eat with us," said the camp boss.

It did no good to say they had eaten. The trappers insisted they eat again. This plan exactly suited Bill. He was happy when his father said they would stay.

He followed the delicious odor straight to the nearest campfire. A trapper was making bread and cooking it. He wrapped dough around a stick. Then he twirled the stick over the blaze until the dough was cooked.

"You can have this one, Bill. Eat it while it's hot. You can have another at supper."

"Thanks, thanks." Bill ate, and that roasted dough did something to him. He knew then and there what his life work would be. He'd be a trapper and catch beaver and make stick bread.

He told the young trapper all this, and then he heard wonderful news.

"I'll teach you to make dough sticks, Bill. I'll be in these parts for a while. I'm going to visit my uncle, Elijah Cody, in Weston."

Mr. Cody had come just in time to hear this. "Then I'm your uncle also," he said, "your Uncle Isaac."

"Well, well! I didn't know you were out here. I'm Horace Billings."

"Of course. I knew when you came west several years ago. Horace, this is your cousin Bill."

"I'm mighty glad you're my cousin, Bill. I took a liking to you the minute I saw you."

"Can't you come home with us, Horace? We're leaving in the morning."

"Why, yes, and thank you, Uncle Isaac. The other men are going on to Leavenworth with their furs."

Around the campfire that evening Mr. Cody told the story of the four red wool blankets. And to his surprise every one of the twenty trappers shouted with laughter.

"Did the braves make terrible faces, Bill?" the boss asked.

"Yes, sir. They scared me."

"They would scare anyone. We know them, Mr. Cody." He turned to the others. "It was Eagle, Lamb, and Fox, I'm sure."

"Yes! Yes!" cried the others, and they laughed again.

"They hunted with us for a month or so," the boss went on. "They were always playing jokes."

"They didn't like this chief of the Kickapoos," said a trapper. "He wouldn't let them hunt on his tribe's land."

"Let's play a joke on them," Horace suggested. "Let's get the blankets."

"Ha, ha! That's the thing! Ha, ha!" laughed others.

"Who will go? Hands up!"

Every hand went up.

"You can't all go," declared the boss. "We need guards here. I'll have your wagon guarded, too, Mr. Cody. I'll arrange everything. And if I know Horace Billings, you'll get your blankets back very soon."

OFF TO THE RESCUE!

There were ten in the rescue party, including Mr. Cody and Bill. They were riding on the trail to Leavenworth. The trappers were certain the Indians would be going to sell their furs.

"They'll stop on the way to hunt," added Horace.

"For fun?" asked Bill.

"No, Indians don't hunt for fun. They hunt only when they need food," a trapper replied.

"It's about eleven o'clock now," said another. "If they had any luck hunting, they'll be in camp. And that's where we'll catch them."

"We'll find them near a creek and away from

the main trail," offered another. "That's the Indian way."

A little later a thin curl of smoke was discovered in just such a place. Horace dismounted and crept through the brush. Presently he returned smiling and nodded.

The other trappers dismounted. Mr. Cody and Bill were asked to remain on their horses. Bill expected to see the men crash through the bushes with whoops and savage yells.

But, instead, the trappers went to the edge of the brush. They stood in a group and sang:

> Ho, pretty beaver!
> Don't flap your tail at me!
> I came out west to find you.
> I want you on my knee.

There was a rustle in the brush. Then three young braves rushed out laughing and shouting. The next minute they were all hugging one another and talking mixed Indian and English. At last Horace remembered why he had come.

"Are these the Indians, Bill?" he asked.

"Yes." Bill nodded.

"Oh!" cried Eagle. "It's the handsome boy! He said we were handsome, too."

There was a great laugh at this. Then Lamb explained that they meant to pay Mr. Cody for the blankets.

"It was worth many skins just to fool old Black Wolf," said Fox.

Horace now spoke to the braves in Indian language, and they stopped laughing at once. He explained how much Mr. Cody needed the Kickapoo chief's friendship.

The braves nodded to one another. Eagle opened a bundle and took out the four blankets. He gave them to Horace and said they didn't mean to make trouble.

Then the trappers said good-by. And the

braves said they would hunt with them again next year—same place—same time—same good luck, they hoped.

On the way back Horace pointed to a narrow trail. "That's the road to Black Wolf's village. Shall we take it?"

"Yes," replied his uncle. "I want to get rid of these blankets before anything else happens."

The trappers left them here. Only Mr. Cody, Bill, and Horace took the narrow trail.

On the Great Plains

A WEEK or so later, Isaac Cody, Horace Billings and Bill were in the barnyard of the Cody farm near Weston, Missouri. The men were showing Bill how to ride the pony Chief Black Wolf had given him the day they took the blankets to the chief.

Now no one had to teach William Frederick Cody how to ride. He had been riding since he was four. But two weeks ago this pony had been out on the prairie in a herd of wild horses.

Horace had broken it, and today Bill was to try it out. He was on it now, trotting around the yard, and the men were pleased.

Just then two soldiers rode up and stopped. Their saddles squeaked, and their spurs and stirrups rattled. These strange noises frightened the pony. It reared, and Bill was thrown.

His father and cousin ran to him. The soldiers jumped down from their horses. But before anyone could reach Bill, he was on his feet chasing the pony. He caught the bridle and stopped him. He patted the scared animal's neck and talked to him gently. After a moment or so he mounted again and trotted around the yard.

"That's the way to do it!" cried Sergeant Love. "You always have to be gentle with a frightened animal."

Then he explained that he and Corporal Hood had been sent by the commander of Fort Leavenworth. They were to find a young trapper, Horace Billings.

"I am Horace Billings. What's wrong, Sergeant?"

"Plenty, sir, plenty. Some forty of our cavalry horses became scared and stampeded three days ago. They took to the plains, and we can't catch them. So the colonel thought you might be able to help us."

"Me? I'm not a soldier."

"No, but the colonel knows all about you. A good many trappers come to the fort to look around and watch the drills."

Horace smiled. "I've been there many times myself."

"Well," continued the sergeant, "the colonel heard that you were an expert with the lasso. He would call it a favor if you would capture the runaways, Mr. Billings."

"They'll be hard to catch. They probably have joined a herd of wild horses."

"The colonel will pay you ten dollars for every one you bring in."

"That's good pay, Horace," remarked his uncle. "You'd better take the offer."

"I'll go—and I'd like to take Bill along, Uncle Isaac."

"Oh, Pa, may I go? I can ride Prince now. And Horace is teaching me lots of things."

"I know he is—but he may be gone some time—too long for you to be away from home."

"I'll take good care of Bill. It's a chance for him to learn about the plains. I know them like a book."

"We'd better all be learning about them," put in Sergeant Love. "We'll have a war with these Plains Indians as sure as the sun sets this evening. The tribes will join together. They are not going to sit still and watch white men settle on their land."

Corporal Hood nodded. "And it will happen by the time this boy is old enough to carry a gun."

"The government paid the Indians for their land, and they paid a good price, too," declared Isaac Cody.

"That's true," agreed Sergeant Love. "The

56

chiefs are satisfied, but the young men want war. They may be able to force the old chiefs into it."

"I'm afraid you are right," agreed Mr. Cody. "Every plainsman, old and young, will have to fight to protect our settlements."

"That's a fact, sir," nodded the sergeant. "I've heard our colonel say the same words."

"Horace, I've changed my mind. I think Bill ought to go with you. I'm sure his mother will consent when I tell her what these soldiers said."

"I'll report for duty in a couple of hours, Sergeant. I'll have my own horse."

"I'll have mine, too," said Bill.

"Good, good! I forgot to say the colonel will furnish a pack mule and supplies. And he'll send our ferry across for you."

As the soldiers rode away they talked about Bill.

"He's got the makings of a good plainsman, Corporal."

"Well, Bill, it looks as if we won't sleep two nights in the same camp from now on. That herd is traveling farther west all the time."

"Do you still think a wild horse is leading it?"

"I do. He's cunning, too."

"You have eighteen horses. That isn't so bad, is it?"

"Very bad for a week's work. I should have had all of them."

"You'll get them."

"I'm not so sure. The wild horse is leading them up into the mountains where I can't lasso them. And he knows it."

"The colonel won't blame you, will he?"

"Of course not. And that reminds me—soldiers are coming today for the captured horses. I can't leave camp so it will be a good time for lessons. How about making a map of the place where we camped yesterday?"

58

Bill began to draw on the ground with a branch from a bush nearby. His cousin said nothing until the map was finished.

"You have the dried-up creek in the right place. But you don't show any landmarks for finding the water hole."

"There was a big cottonwood tree at the right of the hole."

"That's the thing to remember. Now, Bill, how far was this hole from the last one?"

"I think you said three miles."

"Three! I said eight."

"Oh, well, five miles isn't far on the plains."

"That's where you're wrong, Bill. An extra five miles might mean the difference between life and death.

"Suppose you were a scout, and you were guiding an army across these plains. And suppose that each soldier had only enough water in his canteen for one more drink.

"You said the next water hole was three miles
distant. So their officers allowed them to empty
their canteens. Then you found you had made
a terrible mistake. It was eight miles farther,
under a blazing sun. What would happen then?"

"They would suffer from thirst."

"Worse than that, Bill. Many would fall exhausted and die."

"It would be my fault."

"Absolutely, all your fault."

"A scout has to know a lot of things."

"He can't do any guessing, that's certain."

"I'm going to be careful from now on, Horace. I'm going to remember what you tell me."

"Good boy! Then I'll be helping to train another Kit Carson."

"Who? Me?"

"You, William Frederick Cody."

"Well, if I thought I could be like him, I'd be a scout. Horace, could Kit Carson make stick bread?"

"All trappers and scouts learn that. But I'm sure he couldn't make it any better than you do. No one could beat that stick bread you made for dinner today."

Bill was delighted. And again he made up his mind to be a trapper, or a scout. Dough sticks always made him decide something, they smelled so good.

A BUFFALO STAMPEDE

The soldiers had gone with the eighteen horses. And now the cousins were on the way to a new camp farther west.

"I told you this wild horse was smart, Bill. Why doesn't he lead the horses east? Why must he always go west?"

"We'll be so far west pretty soon we can hunt beaver."

Horace laughed. Then almost at once he became serious. "Look, Bill, over to the northwest. What do you see?"

"Nothing but the sand-colored plain and brown sage bushes."

"That brown isn't sage. It's a herd of buffaloes. It's moving this way, and it's moving fast. Something has frightened the beasts."

It wasn't long till Bill could see them, and he was delighted. "We'll be close to them, won't we, Horace? We'll ride right in with them, won't we?"

"Indeed we won't! It's a stampede! We'll get out of their way."

"Can't we watch them pass by?"

"Too dangerous. They might change their direction and come straight down on us."

"Couldn't we stay till they are almost here? Our horses are fast."

"No! I'm not taking any chances."

"You would if you were alone."

"Maybe, but I'm not alone. I have a little greenhorn with me."

"I know a lot about buffaloes."

"All right, Buffalo Bill, I'm glad you do. But

I'm responsible for you. I promised your mother and father I'd take good care of you. Come on. We'll get out of this danger and fast."

Bill was disappointed. He wanted to be so close to the shaggy creatures he could touch them. He obeyed his cousin, however, without another word.

It was almost dark when Bill and Horace made camp by a water hole. Their supper was a quick one—dried meat and parched corn. They always carried a supply of these kinds of food in their saddlebags.

"We'll hunt tomorrow," said Horace. "There'll be plenty of animals around this water hole."

Bill was too sleepy to answer. He rolled his two blankets closely about him, for the nights were cold on the plains. In almost the next minute he was dreaming.

He was riding buffalo in a herd. He was standing and stepping from one to another.

A great many people were watching him. They were clapping their hands and shouting to him. "Buffalo Bill!" they called. "Go on! Go on, Buffalo Bill!"

All of a sudden he wasn't riding. He was sinking down into Buffalo fur—down—down—soft and warm—soft and warm——

Horace had to shake Bill hard the next morning. "Get up! Get up!" he said. "There're flapjacks and honey for breakfast."

"Honey?" Bill was wide-awake now—he loved honey. "I'll be ready in two minutes, Horace. Say, I had a funny and exciting dream last night——"

THE PRAIRIE-DOG VILLAGE

The two hunters found prairie hens close by, enough for the day. Then Horace rode out on the plains, searching for the herd of horses.

Bill went to work on his lessons. On the ground he drew a map of the country around this water hole. He practiced shooting at a target. He was trying to lasso a sage bush when his cousin came back.

"Those horses have given me the slip again," Horace complained. "But I discovered something, Bill. There's a prairie-dog village about five miles from here."

"Really? When can I see it? You'll take me there, won't you? I've been wanting to see one all my life."

"We're going now. Get your pony."

They were within two miles of the place when Horace discovered a horse in the distance. He thought it was close to the dog village.

After a while he said there was something strange about it. The horse hadn't moved since he first saw it.

Bill couldn't see it at all. He hadn't had his

cousin's long experience of looking at faraway objects on the plains. Horace's eyes were as good as field glasses.

"That horse is in the village!" Horace now exclaimed. "I can see the mounds around it. I'm afraid it has stepped into one of those dog tunnels and can't get out."

"The tunnels are deep, aren't they?"

"About fourteen feet, and they go straight down from the hole in the top of each mound. The village is honeycombed with them."

They were close enough now to hear the dogs barking. "It sounds as if there were a hundred," Bill said.

"More like a thousand. This village is very large. It covers acres and acres."

"They don't sound exactly like dogs."

"They aren't dogs. They belong to the squirrel family and have bushy tails. I think they bark like foxes. We'll stop here, Bill. We can't risk our horses any nearer. I'll walk over and see what's wrong with that poor animal."

Bill watched his cousin pick his way carefully as he approached the village. He saw him reach the horse and bend down as if examining its legs.

After a few minutes Bill heard a shot and saw the horse fall.

"I had to shoot him," Horace explained. "His leg was broken, and there was no way to get him out of the tunnel. He was an army horse. He had been shod."

They walked along the edge of the village but well on the outside. Bill was amazed. As far as he could see were small mounds of earth, and on top of each sat a prairie dog yipping and yapping for dear life.

The boy laughed. "It's the funniest thing I've ever seen, Horace. Do they go on like this all the time?"

"All day long. They are just talking to one another."

"About us?"

"Right now, yes. But they'll talk on after we leave."

"Won't I have something to tell when we get back home!"

"I hope I will—I hope I can tell about getting the rest of the horses."

It happened that way. Horace finally captured the others. The colonel was very grateful. He even wanted to pay for the horse that was shot, but Horace refused to accept this.

"I was only helping the poor animal, Colonel. I don't take pay for that."

This was another lesson for William Cody. And it was one he never forgot.

Salt Creek Valley

It was late fall, and Bill was lonely. His father was busy on the farm. His cousin Horace had gone to the Far West to hunt beaver.

His older sisters were too busy to play with him. Martha was only twelve and Julie only ten, but they had to help their mother with the work.

His younger sisters were too young, six and four. And a boy who had been riding the plains couldn't be expected to play baby games.

There were no boys of his age in the neighborhood. Bill had to ride Prince alone and fish and swim alone. It wasn't much fun.

Then suddenly he had a dozen playmates. Their families came in big wagons, little wagons, on horseback and afoot. They camped in the fields around Weston.

It happened almost overnight, and they had all come for the same reason. They wanted that rich land in Salt Creek Valley for farms and homes. Now they had a chance to get it.

The Indians had just sold it to the United States Government. The government was going to sell it to anyone who would settle there. But the buyer had to go there first and drive a stake in the land he wanted. This made it his "claim.

The sale would begin in a short time. The exact date would be in the Weston newspaper. In the meantime the settlers got as close to Kansas as they could.

The Missouri River was the border line. Soldiers from Fort Leavenworth patrolled the shore to see that no one tried to cross secretly.

Isaac Cody waited on the Missouri side with the others. He wanted the land where his trade wagon had stood, but he had to take a chance. Someone with a faster horse might stake the claim first.

So while everyone in the camp waited, Bill was busy making friends there. He played with all the boys of his age, but his best friends were the two Pavey boys, Charlie and Tommy. He told them about his cousin and their trip to the Great Plains. He described the wonderful sights he had seen—the prairie-dog village, the buffaloes, wild horses, water holes, and a dozen other things.

The Pavey boys told other boys, and, before long, Bill was a hero. Every time he went to the camp, boys would beg him to tell them about the plains.

Bill liked to please his friends, so he told them everything. He didn't leave a thing out.

He even added a few extra buffaloes every time he told his dream.

One rainy day he was in the Pavey tent playing with Charlie and Tommy. There were also some new boys, and they wanted to hear Bill's stories.

So, just to oblige, Bill began: "One day I was riding over the plains with my cousin when suddenly, far off in the distance, the ground changed color. It became brown, a dark brown.

" 'Buffalo!' cried my cousin. 'A great herd of them!' I looked and what did I see?"

"Buffaloes!" cried Charlie and Tommy.

"That's right. Nothing but buffaloes as far as I could see, miles and miles and miles. Why, the ground shook just like an earthquake. And their bellowing sounded like thunder."

"That's not so!" cried a voice at the tent flap. "You didn't see any buffaloes!"

It was that bully from Weston, Abel Smith's

son—that big, redheaded, mean Jake Smith. He didn't belong to Bill's crowd. He was all of fifteen. But the older boys wouldn't play with him. They said he was always trying to start a fight. The younger boys were afraid of him.

"He's making up those stories just so you'll call him Buffalo Bill," the bully went on.

"I am not!"

"You are, too! I'll fight anyone that says you aren't. And I'll fight anybody that calls you Buffalo Bill, too. Go on and try it. Go on!"

The boys were silent.

"Scared to, aren't you? You'd better be. Walking on top of a thousand buffaloes! Stepping across them! It's all a pack of lies."

"I dreamed that," said Bill.

"I don't believe you. And my pa says there isn't any prairie-dog town like you are always bragging about seeing."

"I saw it myself. So did my cousin."

"You didn't!"

"He did! He did!" cried the Pavey boys.

"I'll fight anybody that says he did. Come on! I'm ready for you!"

"You'll fight me first," said Bill. "I'm ready for you."

Just then Mrs. Pavey came into the tent. She

had heard the boys' angry voices outside. And now, when she saw their angry faces, she was alarmed. "Boys," she said quickly, "it has stopped raining, and I need the tent. You'll have to go now."

As they left she asked Bill in a low tone to stay. A little later she went home with him and told his parents what had happened. "I was afraid Jake would wait for Bill and hurt him. He bullies Bill all the time. My boys tell me about it."

"I think I understand the reason," Isaac Cody said gravely. "My brother Elijah told me just yesterday. He said this boy's father, Abel Smith, was to blame. It seems Abel is angry at me because he wants the land I have selected over in Kansas."

"Well, let him get there first then," declared Mrs. Pavey. "He has to run a chance the same as you."

"Of course. I expect it will be a race between Abel and me."

"May I go with you?" asked Bill.

"No, son, it will be too dangerous for a boy. The ferryboats will be crowded. And on the trail the men will be excited and riding hard. They might push you over the side of a hill and not know they had done it."

"They wouldn't have a chance. My pony is the fastest horse in Weston. And Horace said I could ride like a Sioux Indian."

"Yes, and he said you could yell like a Kickapoo," said his mother. "But you are going to mind like an eight-year-old. You are not going."

"Yes, Ma."

LIVING ON A BUSY TRAIL

Isaac Cody won the race! He was driving his stake when Abel Smith came.

"I'll run you out!" the man shouted angrily. "You'll see what will happen to you!"

Mr. Cody paid no attention. He was clearing his land one day, and Bill was helping. Bill helped get the logs ready for the cabin, too, but he couldn't help raise them. The neighbors did this. Mr. Pavey came from his farm two miles away. Others came three or four miles. Mr. Cody had already helped them, they said.

The cabin stood where the trade wagon had been six months before. It faced the main trail and had a pretty front yard. The whole Cody family was delighted.

There was so much to see! There were still settlers in big covered wagons and gold seekers. Hunters, trappers, fur traders, and Indians used this trail. And sometimes the marshal and his posse rode by.

As if this wasn't enough excitement, something else happened. One morning four Kicka-

poo families from Missouri put up their tepees only a mile away. Before night Bill had discovered three boys his age, Badger, Beaver, and Bear. Then the fun began. The four boys rode their ponies all over the prairie. They swam and fished and hunted small game.

They picked berries and gathered nuts for their mothers. They explored caves and played in Mr. Cody's big wagon. The boys taught Bill to shoot with bow and arrows. They taught him Indian games and Kickapoo words.

He went to their camp every day or so. Sometimes he ate there, but not unless he was invited by his friends' parents. Bill had learned a good deal about Indian politeness.

"They have good manners," he told his folks.

"You must ask the boys here, Bill," said Mrs. Cody. "I'll get a nice dinner for them."

"They are bashful with strangers. I don't think they will come."

"Try to persuade them. Tell them one week from today. Can you make them understand?"

Bill nodded. "I know some Kickapoo, and they know some English. We make out."

"Isaac," said Mary that evening, "what do you think about inviting the boys' fathers and mothers, too? They have been so good to Bill."

"I think it's just the thing to do. I'd like to get acquainted with them myself."

"There's one thing about Bill, Isaac—he makes good friends."

The very next day Bill was sick. "Measles," said his mother. "The Pavey boys were down with it when you were there Saturday. You caught it from them."

"I have to go to Fort Leavenworth this morning with the Indian boys. We want to watch the cavalry drill."

"You can't go anywhere for a while, Bill. We can't have the dinner now—not for three weeks anyway."

"I don't feel very bad."

"You have a little fever, and your face is broken out with a rash."

"Oh, well, I don't mind that. Leavenworth isn't very far."

"Look here, Bill, do you want your friends to catch measles from you? They might be very sick. Medicine men don't know how to cure this disease."

82

Bill sighed. "I guess I'd better stay in. I don't want to give it to anyone."

"Bill! Bill! Bill!" called the voices from the front yard.

Martha peeped out the window. "It's the Indians—on their ponies."

Mrs. Cody went outside at once. She greeted the boys pleasantly and then told them Bill was sick.

Their smiling young faces became grave. "Very sick?" asked Bear.

"He has the measles. His face is broken out." "His face is broken?" asked Beaver. "His nose?"

"He didn't break his face. It's just broken out. Rash—red rash."

The boys shook their heads. This English puzzled them.

"Broken arm!" exclaimed Badger. "That's bad."

"Very bad," said Bear with a nod.

They talked together for a moment. Then they turned to Mrs. Cody.

"We'll be back," said Beaver. "We'll bring the medicine man to fix Bill."

They rode away quickly. And now it was Mary Cody who was puzzled. She didn't know what to do. She told Bill she didn't. "If we refuse to let him see you, your friends will feel bad. If we let him come in, you'll be scared into a high fever."

"He won't scare me. I've seen him wear his mask. I've heard him shake his rattles, too, over a sick boy."

"I'll see what your father says. Now eat this milk toast while it's hot."

Bill ate and then went to sleep. He was awakened later on by strange noises outside. They were made by a drum and bone rattles.

Mrs. Cody came in. "Bill, he is here, and he looks terrible. His mask is frightful."

"I don't care, I want him to come in. The boys
will worry about me if he doesn't."

"All right then, but we'll be in here, too. You
won't be alone with him."

She opened the door and beckoned. Mr. Cody
entered first. He was followed by the medicine
man wearing a frightful mask. He made a few
motions over Bill's head. Then he danced

around the bed slowly, shaking his bone rattles softly.

All the time a drum was beating out in the yard slowly and softly.

Now the medicine man began to dance faster, and the drumbeats were faster and louder. He whirled around the bed so fast he made Bill dizzy. He rattled the bones fiercely right in Bill's face.

Finally he stopped, and the drum was silent. He gave Bill's hand a kindly pat and left the room. Mr. Cody followed him.

"Your father will thank him," Mrs. Cody said. "And he will thank the boys for bringing him. It shows how much they all think of you."

"Can't I get up now? I want to look out the window."

"No, you can't get up. I'm your medicine man now, and I'll do more than shake rattles if you get out of bed."

"What?"

"I don't know."

They both laughed. Then Bill said he was hungry and wanted some more milk toast.

"Good-by, Bill! Good-by, Bill! Good-by, Bill!" called his friends from the yard.

The patient smiled. It was nice to have friends, very nice.

Horse Thieves

In two years the Cody farm was in good shape.
Cattle were in the pasture. Horses were in the
big log barn. Hay and corn were in the fields.

Everything was going along very well, and
everyone was happy. Then came bad news.
Abel Smith had bought the farm adjoining the
Cody's on the south. He had moved into the
cabin with his family.

"Where is Bill?" asked Mary Cody the instant
she heard this.

"I let him off today to go fishing. He has been
working hard. I thought he needed a rest."

"Is he alone?"

"He was to meet the Pavey boys at Deer Creek."

"I'm glad. He must not go any place alone now, Isaac."

"At least not until we find what kind of neighbors the Smiths are."

"I think we know. How could he buy this farm? He didn't have a cent when he lived in Weston. And he didn't work."

"There was something strange about that. Elijah thought he belonged to a gang of horse thieves."

"Why does he come here if he won't farm?"

"There's just one answer to that, Mary. He expects to get money some other way."

"It will be bad for Bill."

"It may be bad for all of us. He may be still angry because I got this land."

"I've often wondered why he was so anxious to get it."

"It would make a splendid hideout for a gang of horse thieves—much better than the place he bought. We have a deep ravine where stolen horses could be hidden."

"That's the reason, of course! That explains everything."

At this very moment Bill had reached Deer Creek, but the Pavey boys hadn't come. Oh, well, they would be along pretty soon. They wouldn't miss a chance to fish here, and they couldn't come without him.

Deer Creek was on Kickapoo land, but the chief had given Bill permission to fish here. "Bring your friends," the chief had said. "You're a good boy."

It was too bad the Kickapoo boys had gone back to Missouri. They would like this place. It was splendid for trout. Bill caught a big one almost at once. He was baiting his hook again when he heard a noise.

He turned, expecting to see Charlie and Tommy. He saw Jake Smith!

"Caught you, didn't I? You haven't any business on Indian land."

"The chief told me I could fish here."

"I don't believe it. Get out!"

"I won't! You can't make me."

"I'll show you." He threw the fish into the creek. "How do you like that?" he sneered. "And I've a good mind to throw you in."

"I can swim."

"I'll fix you so you can't do anything."

Bill was really frightened, but he had courage. "You'd better not hurt me. My father will get the marshal after you."

"Marshal, pooh! I'm not afraid of him. He can't do anything to me. My pa said so. Pa's got more men than the marshal. I can treat you any way I want. And I'm going to finish you up right now. I'm going to!"

He started toward Bill with clenched fists.

Bill opened his mouth and gave the Kickapoo war whoop. He had a voice that could be heard a half mile if he just called. His war whoop was good for a mile and maybe more.

"Shut that up!" yelled Jake.

Bill didn't shut up. He whooped again and Jake hit him. Bill fell.

Then came war whoops from the trees close by. Three Indian hunters rushed out and down to the creek. Jake ran for his life.

Bill got up slowly with the help of the Indians. He said he wasn't hurt, but his head felt dizzy.

"You whoop good," said one Indian.

"I thought you were an Indian," said another smiling.

"We'll take you home," offered the third. "I'm Red Eye, and your father's our friend. He showed me how to farm."

On the way the hunter gave Bill advice.

"Keep away from that boy. He's bad, and his father's bad, too. He stole my pony.

Now the Pavey boys joined Bill and Red Eye, but the Indian wouldn't leave till Bill was in his own yard.

THE THUNDER OF HOOFS MEANT TROUBLE

One morning soon after this, Mr. Cody found his pasture fence had been broken down. Some of his cattle had wandered away, and he had a hard time finding them. Two days later he found the corn trampled down in his field.

Each time he traced footprints and hoofprints. They led straight to the Smith farm. Now he knew what kind of neighbor he had. That night he learned still more.

It was moonlight, and he happened to be in the barnyard when he saw a band of men riding by. He hid behind a tree and watched. They turned into the Smith lane.

"Someone will lose horses tonight," he told

his wife. "I'm sure I saw the gang of horse thieves."

He was right. A neighbor's horses were stolen. He knew his turn would come and it did. One night he heard the thunder of hoofs. The next morning his cattle were gone.

Another night his corncrib was burned, and all his grain was stolen.

"They mean to drive us away, Mary. They'll stop at nothing."

"Surely the marshal will arrest them. It can't go on like this."

The marshal didn't arrest anyone. In the next few nights riders burned barns and stole cattle and horses all over the valley. People were terrified and began to move away.

Elijah came and advised his relatives to leave, but Mary refused. "I will not be driven out of my own home," she said.

Even after most of their horses had been

taken, she still refused. Then Isaac went to the marshal.

"I wish I could arrest those rascals," the officer declared. "But I can't get enough men for a posse. Everyone is afraid. The settlers know what these riders would do to them and their families."

Mr. Cody nodded. "They'd take revenge. I know that, for I know some of them. They meet at the Smith farm. I hear them passing every few nights."

"Keep out of the way, Mr. Cody. Don't let a light show in your cabin. Make them think you are all sound asleep. They don't want people to know who they are."

"My family is terrified. Surely you can do something. We must have law and order."

"I keep hoping I can find men who are willing to risk it. Now be careful on your way home, Mr. Cody. They have never attacked anyone in daytime, but they're getting so bold we don't know what will happen."

Isaac had reached the steep hill when he saw several men come out of the woods. Only one was riding, but they all carried guns, and Abel Smith was one of them. They deliberately blocked the trail, and Smith seized the bridle of Mr. Cody's horse and held it. "You've been talking to the marshal," he said angrily. "No use to deny it. That man just told us."

"I saw you!" cried the man on the horse. "I saw you when you went into his office."

"What did you tell the marshal?" asked Abel.

Mr. Cody was silent.

"I reckon you named names to him," Abel went on.

Mr. Cody was still silent.

"Talk! Talk!" they all yelled.

"All right, I'll talk. I said it was time we had law and order in this valley."

There was a loud report, a flash of fire, and
Isaac Cody fell from his horse. The men ran
into the brush and disappeared.

A neighbor found Mr. Cody an hour later and brought him home in his wagon. Isaac wasn't badly hurt. He had been shot in the leg, and it was just a flesh wound.

"The riders will be after me again," he said, "as soon as they know I'm still alive. You must hide me."

Mrs. Cody decided the cornfield was the best place, so the sick man was carried there. He was made comfortable, and Bill stayed with him and brought his meals. They spoke in whispers, for the farm was being watched by the Smith gang.

The Indian, Red Eye, had come secretly to the Cody farm to tell this. But Mary Cody knew she could trust Bill to manage his trips to the field. She had seen him disappear into that forest of tall corn almost without a sound. There was only a faint rustle of long green leaves such as a little breeze would make.

Indeed, no Indian scout, not even the great Carson himself, could have been more cautious and careful.

"Don't worry, Pa," Bill whispered. "They won't find you."

"Bill," whispered his father, "you would make a good scout. You think things out before you act."

The neighbor came back the second night with his wagon and took Isaac to his brother's home in Weston. Mrs. Cody knew he would be safe there.

Ruffians came to the cabin the very next day. They demanded Mr. Cody. They searched the house and barn. They threatened the family. They smashed furniture. They took food. And, worst of all, they took Bill's pony, Prince.

Only one bright thing happened in those dark days. Prince got away and came back.

Mr. Cody recovered, but he didn't dare come

back home to live. The night riders were still riding. So he bought a sawmill at Grasshopper Falls, Kansas, and did very well. Once in a while he came back home, but only at night, and secretly.

One morning the Indian, Red Eye, came to see Mrs. Cody again. He had heard white men talk yesterday. They said they would go to the Falls for Mr. Cody.

"Did they say when?" Mrs. Cody asked.

"Yes. They're starting now, today. Someone must warn Mr. Cody. He's a fine man and a good friend to me."

Bill was the only one who could go, but it would be a very dangerous journey. The boy wouldn't listen to his mother's fears. He mounted Prince and was off.

Nothing happened until he was halfway there. He came suddenly upon five men at a creek. They had stopped to water their horses and had dismounted.

One of them knew Bill. "It's Cody's son!" Bill heard him say. Then they all yelled at him to stop.

Bill whipped his pony and rode past them. They shot at him, but the bullets went wild. Before they could mount, he had a good start. He rode like the wind.

Presently he heard them coming. They had big strong horses. They would overtake him in time. He knew this, but he didn't worry about himself. He must warn his father. He must!

If only help would come! And suddenly help came. There was a thunderstorm with lightning and pouring rain.

The men stopped for shelter, but Bill rode on. He was drenched. He was cold, and his teeth chattered. He could hardly sit in the saddle. But he went on.

Finally he reached the sawmill. He warned his father. Then he fell into Mr. Cody's arms.

"You're a brave boy," Isaac said. And there were tears in his eyes. Bill had risked his life for him.

Bill was put to bed and kept there the rest of the day. Early the next morning, Mr. Cody and Bill left the Falls for a new place of safety, Lawrence, Kansas.

Freighting West

THE FREIGHT yards of the Russell, Majors and Waddell Far-West Freight Company were just outside Leavenworth, Kansas. They made a wonderful sight. There was nothing like the yards in the world, for the trains were made up of big covered wagons.

Great warehouses were filled with all kinds of supplies—mostly ammunition, food, and clothing—for the Far West forts. The wagons were loaded here, and the trains started from here.

There were acres of wagons and acres of wheels, axles, ox yokes, and white canvas covers.

There were hundreds of employees—loaders,

drivers, blacksmiths, wheelwrights, hunters, and cavy, or herd drivers, wagon masters, camp bosses, and yardmen.

A thousand mules brayed. A thousand oxen lowed. Horses neighed. Dogs barked. Busy men were everywhere.

Freighting was a big business. Wagon trains were leaving every few days. And there was always a crowd to see them start, although it was at daybreak. There were people from the town and soldiers from Fort Leavenworth, a mile or so away.

The wagon train looked like a fleet of ships sailing out to sea, people said—and just as dangerous.

One day in the spring of 1857, a yard boss entered Mr. Major's office. He said a boy wanted to see him about getting a job.

"No boys, Sam. I need a man for cavy herder. That's the only thing open."

"This boy is a wonderful rider, Mr. Majors. We watched him as he rode up."

"Is that so? Who is he?"

"Bill Cody, from Salt Creek Valley."

"I know his father. Let him come in, Sam."

Presently Bill came in with his gun on his arm. He smiled and said good morning. Then he stood quietly with his hat in his hand.

Mr. Majors liked him at once for his nice manners. He liked the keen, smart look in the boy's eyes, too. Then he told Bill to sit down and tell him why he had come.

"I have to find work, Mr. Majors. I have to support my family now. My father died a month ago."

"I didn't know that. I'm sorry—he was a fine man. I knew there was a lot of trouble with night riders."

"They were the cause of his death. He caught cold hiding from them."

"Too bad, too bad! He had a good farm in the valley. Your mother has that, of course."

"Yes, but we haven't anything to farm with. The riders stole everything."

"I'm glad the army got those rascals. They are all in prison now, I think."

"Yes, sir, they are—Abel Smith among them. They let his son off."

"I see. Well, Bill, I heard you could ride. Can you shoot? I mean, you must be extra good. Every one of our drivers and helpers must be a fine marksman."

"I'll show you." He took up his gun. "See that bird flying?" He shot through the open door, and the bird fell.

"Splendid! You do have keen eyes. How old are you?"

"Eleven. But I'm tall. I look twelve. Everyone says so."

"You do look twelve."

"I'm strong, too. I helped my father clear land."

"Yes, you look strong."

"I can stay in the saddle all day. I've done it many times, herding cattle."

Mr. Majors shook his head. "You are too young to drive a herd behind the wagon train. Do you know what you would have to do?"

"Keep all the extra horses, mules, and oxen in line and going west."

"And they won't keep in line, and they won't go west if they can help it. They are afraid of strange country."

"I know," nodded Bill. "They get homesick for their old pastures. But they get over that the second day out."

"Yes, they do. I see you understand animals. Well, I might use you, but you'll have to do a man's work."

"Of course. I'd expect to, sir."

"I would pay you a man's wages, fifty dollars for the trip."

"Fifty dollars! Mr. Majors, I've got to work for you. We're out of money at home. And if anything happens to me, I want my pay to go to my mother."

"Wait a minute—you're not hired yet. There's one more thing I have to know. Did your mother consent to this work?"

The boy hesitated. "Well—we—we talked it over——"

"And she refused, didn't she?"

Bill nodded. "She's afraid of Indians."

"There is danger if there are only a few wagons. But our trains have from ten to twenty-five. Our teamsters and hunters are dead shots, and the Indians know it. They don't attack us very often. We always drive them off."

"That's what I told her, but she wouldn't listen."

110

"So you came anyway."

"Yes, sir. I knew I had to find work."

"Well, go back home and try again. I won't take you unless you bring your mother's consent in writing."

That afternoon Bill came back with Mary Cody's written consent. "I promised I'd go to school as soon as we get one out there in the valley," he explained.

"All right, Bill, you're hired. Now I ask all of our men to sign a pledge. Read it and sign here, if you agree to it."

The boy's face turned red. "I can't read or write," he stammered. "I—I've never gone to school."

"Why, of course not! There weren't any schools in the valley. Well, this pledge says you will not be cruel to the animals in any way. Can you promise this?"

"I can. I can't bear to see any animal mistreated. My father couldn't either."

"Good. Now make an X here. I'll write your name under it."

TROUBLES ON THE TRAIL

Bill Cody's first job began at dawn when the wagon master called, "Stretch out!"

At once twenty-five great white covered wagons began to fall in line and stretch out over the prairies. They were heavily loaded with supplies for soldiers in Far Western forts.

Each was drawn by an eight-mule team or by six oxen. And each was driven by an experienced plainsman with a pistol in his belt. His gun was on the seat beside him.

Back of the wagons straggled the extra animals: horses, mules, and oxen. Back of them rode the cavy boy, Bill Cody, on a little gray mule. He swung a knotted rope in his hand to keep the beasts in line.

Mr. Majors had told the truth. These animals not only wanted to go back, they were determined to go. They kept the cavy boy busy all day long.

The second day they didn't try to go home, but they spread out and disappeared over low hills. Bill chased them all day again.

This wasn't half his troubles. Sometimes the

dust was so thick he could hardly breathe. Sometimes it rained hard for hours. But he had to keep his herd together no matter what happened.

He was glad when night came, and he could rest by the campfire. But he didn't complain, and the men liked him for this.

The wagons were placed in a big circle every night. It was the best way to meet an Indian attack. The mules, oxen, and extra animals were tethered just outside where they could graze. The cook wagon was inside, and the men slept under the wagons.

Every man did his share of guard duty. Bill stood guard every third night, outside the circle, alone in the dark, listening every instant for suspicious noises. He was watching constantly for shadowy figures of enemies.

Of course he was scared, but he didn't complain. He had been hired to do a man's job, and he'd do it. The men liked him for this, too. Bill Cody was making friends.

ATTACKED BY SIOUX

One noon the train halted on the bank of a creek. The wagons were not in a circle—it didn't seem necessary. They wouldn't stop long, and not an Indian had been seen.

The crew was resting while the cook was getting dinner. Three lookouts had been posted, but no one even thought of danger.

Suddenly there were three shots. Bill saw the guards fall. Then he saw a large band of Indians with painted faces charging down on the camp.

"Run to the creek! Keep under the bank!" shouted the camp boss.

Bill ran with the others. The plainsmen fired from this position and were able to stop the warriors for a moment.

"They outnumber us two to one," said the boss. "Go up the creek! Make for Fort Kearney! Hold them off! Keep shooting!"

They waded up the creek, firing as they went. It was all Bill could do to keep up with them. The water was waist-high for him. He didn't have the strength to shoot.

After hours of wading the party came out on

the other shore. Their shots had been accurate. A good many warriors had been killed, and the others kept a safe distance. Now it was dusk. It wasn't likely the enemy would follow them any farther. So they stopped to take care of the wounded.

No one noticed that Bill was missing. He couldn't keep up with them. He had left the creek, but he was some distance below, on the opposite shore.

If he called, the Indians would know where he was. He didn't know what to do. But he kept in dark shadows and walked softly.

Suddenly he saw a warrior on the bank just above him. The Indian was looking at the white men on the other shore and hadn't seen Bill.

The warrior bent his bow. He was preparing to kill one of Bill's friends. The boy was horrified. He raised his rifle and fired.

The Indian fell over the bank almost at his

feet. Some of the party hurried back. They had missed Bill and heard the shot almost at the same time.

"You saved one of us from death," a driver said.

"That was a mighty good shot," a hunter added. "Your bullet hit his heart."

Then the plainsmen hurried on, but now some of them were always close to Bill. It was dawn when they reached Fort Kearney. Everyone was exhausted.

The next eastbound wagon train took them back to Leavenworth. Bill went home with his wages, proud as a peacock.

"Fifty dollars, Ma!" he shouted. "Fifty dollars for you!"

In School
and Out

Salt Creek Valley was to have a school at last. The log house had been built. School would begin next week, and the teacher was to come any day now.

Mrs. Cody was pleased. Her children would have a chance to learn something. She would send the three oldest, Martha, Julia, and Bill. That fifty dollars would pay the teacher and buy books and winter clothing.

The girls were excited. They could hardly wait for the first day. Bill didn't say anything, but he wasn't happy about it.

To shut him up in a schoolroom when he

could be galloping over the prairie! To make him sit on a bench when he could be listening to stories at a campfire! Every man had some narrow escape to tell. Just in the nick of time each had been saved from Indians, outlaws, bears, wolves, or blizzards. He couldn't give up all this.

There was a freight train out of Leavenworth next week. Mr. Majors had told him he could always have some kind of work, whenever he wanted to go. Maybe he could talk his mother into it.

"It's a good chance to make money, Ma. It's a two-month trip, all the way to Utah. I'll get forty dollars a month. That will be eighty dollars. Just think of that! Eighty dollars for you and the girls!"

"We can get along without it. I'll rent the farm, and you can keep us in meat. You're a good hunter."

"I might get sick. Or it might storm so I couldn't hunt. Or——"

"I won't listen to any more excuses. Your father wanted you to go to school, Bill. He would feel ashamed if he knew you couldn't even write your name."

Bill said no more. He was ashamed of that X mark himself. Well, he'd go to school and get it over with. It was like having measles.

Then came news that changed everything. The teacher couldn't come! So when the wagon train "stretched out" the next week, young Cody was herding the extra animals.

Two months passed, but Bill didn't come home. Three months passed, but Bill didn't come home. Three months—four. Then he came, thin, pale, and weak. Yes, he had been sick with fever and a cough. All the men had been sick with colds. But they had received their full wages. Here were Bill's, one hundred and sixty dollars.

"Mr. Majors paid us for every day we were out," he explained. "And we weren't working at all for two months. We were resting at Fort Bridger."

"Why were you there?" asked Mrs. Cody. "That Fort isn't in Utah. And why did you need to rest so long? What happened, Bill?"

Then Bill told the story. They had almost reached Utah with the supplies for the soldiers there. They were making their noontime halt one day when they were suddenly surrounded by enemies.

"Indians!" cried Martha and Julia.

"No, outlaws—white men, but they were just as bad as Indians."

The wagons and supplies were seized, but Bill and his friends were allowed to keep their arms and some food. After a long and weary march, they reached Fort Bridger. They waited there for the next eastbound train.

Winter had come, and it had been so stormy the wagons couldn't travel. But the men needed the two months to rest. Some were in bad shape.

"And you, Bill? What about you?"

"Well, I didn't feel so good, Ma. I wished I was home every day."

The trip back was bad. They had been attacked by Indians twice but had driven them off. They had been almost frozen in a blizzard. Wolves had come too close—their howling was frightful.

Yes, it was nice to be home again. It was so safe and warm. And Mother's meals were certainly better than flapjacks made of moldy flour.

Tears came into Mary Cody's eyes as she listened to the hardships her son had suffered.

"I hope you've had enough of the plains, Bill."

"Well, I'd be willing to go to school."

"You can go. We found another teacher, and the school opened two months ago. Martha and Julia are going. I'll talk to the teacher about you."

"I want to learn to write my name. Mr. Majors said I should."

"I'll arrange for you to start next Monday."

"Maybe we'd better talk it over again. Mr. Majors said I could go with the next train, and maybe I should."

"No, no more talk. You're pretty good at that, and you might talk me into it. You are going to school this time."

The teacher, young Ralph Woods, was from the East, Ohio. He didn't know very much about the West. But he knew enough to dread this new pupil, William Cody.

This boy had been living in camps with rough men and fighting Indians. Why, he was bound to be rude and wild. He'd upset the whole school. He wouldn't study or mind.

So young Mr. Woods was surprised when a handsome, quiet boy came with his two pretty sisters, Martha and Julia Cody. The teacher noticed Bill's good manners at once.

He was more surprised when Bill said he wanted to learn to write. He didn't need to write anything but his name. How long would it take?

"That depends on how much you practice."

"Oh, I'll practice. I'll stay in after school if you want me to."

126

This didn't sound like a boy who wouldn't study. But he seemed to think he could take just one subject, writing.

"You must take reading, spelling, and arithmetic also, William."

"But I only want to write my name!"

"I'll make a bargain with you. I'll agree to teach you to write your name in one week, if you'll agree to study the other subjects, too."

The boy was delighted. Of course he'd study the other things. And he didn't dream he could learn to write that soon. But he did.

In two weeks he was writing his name all over the neighborhood. He used the burned end of a stick and wrote on wagon covers, tents, barn doors, fence rails, and corncribs.

There it was! *Bill Cody—Bill Cody—Bill Cody*.

He was the proudest boy in Kansas. But he didn't forget to be fair. "You kept your word," he told his teacher, "and I'll keep mine." So he studied, and he studied. No one in the school worked harder on reading, spelling, and arithmetic.

He was really getting along very well until one Saturday a month later. The Pavey boys were spending the day with him. Tommy discovered a hickory tree loaded with nuts on the Smith place.

The tree was close to the cabin, but the Smiths weren't there and hadn't been for a long time. So the Paveys thought it would be all right to help themselves.

"Our farm hand told me to stay off that place," Bill said.

"The nuts will just go to waste. We might as well have them," argued the Paveys.

So Bill consented, and over the rail fence they went. While his friends gathered nuts, Bill was writing his name on the cabin door.

"Write Buffalo Bill under it," suggested Charlie. "You know how angry that made Jake."

Bill laughed. "I will, and I wish he were here to see it."

Just then there was a loud noise inside the

cabin, and an angry voice called out, "Stop your writing! Get off this place, or I'll shoot!"

Bill stepped back from the door. He was surprised. "Who's in there?" he called.

The next instant a bullet whizzed through the cabin door, and the boys ran for their lives. They didn't stop till they were under the walnut tree by the side of the Cody barn.

"Who was it, Bill?" asked the boys.

"Abel Smith."

"I thought he was in jail."

"I guess he's out now. He's liable to shoot me on sight."

The Paveys agreed.

"I'd better tell my mother," Bill said. "Let's go to the cabin."

"You can't cross the yard, Bill. He'll see you."

"Maybe he didn't leave the cabin. I'll see if he's in his yard."

Bill climbed the walnut tree. Presently he

came down. He hadn't seen Abel, but he had seen a wagon freight train on the hill going west.

"Oh, well, you can't go," said Charlie. "You're in school."

"I won't be if Abel takes a shot at me."

The Paveys agreed to this also.

"I'm going!"

"Do you mean now?"

"Right now. Mr. Majors said I could always have some kind of work."

"But you'll have to ask your mother and get your clothes and say good-by."

"I won't have time. You boys can tell her. She'll understand. She wouldn't want me to stay here and be killed."

The boys promised, and Bill disappeared in the brush along the trail. A little later they caught glimpses of him as he climbed the steep hill.

They saw the long wagon train passing along

the hilltop trail. Now Bill reached it. The Paveys saw him jump onto a wagon. Then Bill and the wagon disappeared.

"Maybe he'll never come back, Tommy. Indians."

"Or outlaws."

"Or a grizzly bear."

"Or a blizzard."

"Well, come on. Let's tell Mrs. Cody."

At Old Fort Laramie

THIS TIME the train made it! No Indians—no outlaws—no storms—all the way to Wyoming. But in spite of this, every man was delighted when the high white walls of Fort Laramie came into view. They meant safety from the dangers of the trail.

William Cody was surprised at the size of the fort. There were some thirty buildings inside those whitewashed walls. Also a large parade ground, a yard, and stables.

"Look, Bill," said an old driver proudly, "look how clean and neat everything is."

"Look at the grass in the yard, Bill," said the

wagon master. "There isn't a blade out of place."

"Did you ever see such stables, Bill?" asked the blacksmith. "They must scrub them every hour."

"Look at the sentries, Bill," said the camp boss, Lew Simpson. "Notice their white gloves!"

"Away out here! White gloves!" Bill could hardly believe his eyes.

"Yes indeed, away out here. Don't you forget that this is still the United States of America. And up there floats her flag."

Bill looked up and took off his hat. His heart thrilled when he saw the Stars and Stripes floating gently in the breeze.

He was thrilled again when a troop of United States cavalry dashed by. Their uniforms were gorgeous, and their swords flashed in the bright sunlight.

"It's a hard trip out here," Mr. Simpson told

the fort commander. "But it's harder to get the men away. They would stay all summer if they could."

Colonel Munroe smiled. "There are some other folks who like us," he said. "Did you notice that camp by the Laramie River, close to the fort?"

Lew nodded. "We thought they were gold seekers."

"They are, and there's a different bunch every few days. Most of them buy provisions from the settlers' store. But some just help themselves from our supplies."

"Don't you keep a guard over your storehouse?"

"Not always. Just now I can't spare men. There have been a good many desertions this spring."

"Desertions? Away out here? Where would the soldiers go?"

"California, to find gold. They caught the fever from gold seekers, I suppose."

"Soldiers are people after all, Colonel."

"They haven't any right to be people. They swore to protect and defend this fort when they enlisted in the army."

"You are right. It would be bad if the Indians went on the warpath."

"There's always that danger."

"Well, I'm going on with the supplies for Fort Hall. I won't need all my men. I can leave some here if you wish."

"I'd be grateful to you, Mr. Simpson."

So it happened that a tall thin boy of twelve stood guard that night and every night from seven to ten at the fort storehouse.

Bill Cody didn't like guard duty, but he didn't complain. He knew the older men had given him the early hours to favor him. And this was true. They thought the world of him.

As for Bill, he thought the world of everyone in the fort. There was one visitor he was very fond of, Mr. Kit Carson. The wonderful old Indian scout had taken a fancy to Bill, too.

He was teaching Bill the Indian sign language. He was also giving the boy valuable information about the Plains Indians.

"There isn't any white man who knows them so well," declared the commander. "I hope he will stay here all summer and help me talk to these chiefs."

Mr. Carson spoke the language of some of the Plains tribes. For the others he used sign language.

The chiefs had come to complain about white travelers through Indian lands. They said these white men were stealing their ponies. And even worse, the grass on their grazing land was eaten by the white men's oxen, mules, horses, and cattle.

For miles and miles on each side of the long trail, there was hardly a blade of grass now. The Indians had to take their ponies far away for food—a three days' journey from their villages.

Mr. Carson sympathized with the red men. He said they should be paid for the use of their grazing land. He promised to see that they were paid for the stock that had been stolen from them. Young Bill Cody could see how much the chiefs respected this quiet little man. In fact, everyone in the fort respected and admired him.

Every morning Bill watched the soldiers drill on the parade ground. They were away out on the desert, but every gun was polished, and buttons and belts were gleaming.

Then there was the exciting cavalry parade and practice on the plains. Such riding and wheeling and charging! Such galloping with swords held aloft! It was thrilling.

The Indian warriors were thrilled, too, and showed it. There was always a crowd of them watching.

Every day there was something new and interesting. Younger scouts came and went, also fur traders, trappers, hunters, settlers, and gold seekers.

"Won't I have a lot to tell my mother and sisters!" Bill said to himself almost every day. "And I won't forget the sentries' white gloves, either."

BILL'S SIOUX FRIENDS

There was a large camp of Sioux Indians about a mile from the fort. Their chief, Rain-in-the-Face, had come to complain.

He said his warriors wouldn't keep the peace much longer. The white men must stop killing his braves. Maybe a brave did get the wrong cow. Must he be shot?

141

While the colonel and Kit Carson talked with the chief, Bill was getting acquainted with the Sioux boys. He played games with them. He went to the camp. He fished and swam with them.

He rode in their pony races, and he didn't have to ride an army mule either. There was always a good pony for him. His friend Little Wren saw to this, for he was the chief's son.

Bill saw Rain-in-the-Face several times when he visited Little Wren. And always the chief was kind to the white boy. Once he said, "You're a good son, Bill, to work so hard and give your pay to your mother. I know all about it. Kit Carson told me about you.

"Little Wren helps his mother, too. He brings home meat: big game, little squirrels, little rabbits."

Then the chief laughed and patted his boy's head.

"They act just as white people do when they

are at home," Bill told Mr. Carson. "The chief plays with Little Wren just as my father played with me. He jokes, too."

"Of course." Kit nodded. "We're all alike under the skin. It's a pity we can't be better friends."

"I thought we were. We're at peace."

"It won't last. These very Sioux friends may become your enemies. But go on playing with them, Bill. Be a good friend. Show them that some whites can be trusted."

One day Little Wren took Bill to the river shore to see a raft the Indian boys had made. He said they would float down the Laramie River, all the way to the fort.

"You can't do it, Little Wren. The river is too swift. The raft will be dashed on rocks."

"The raft is strong enough, and so are we."

Then it all happened so quickly, Bill didn't have a chance to say any more. Four boys with long poles jumped on the raft. One of them was Little Wren.

At the same time other boys pushed the raft out from the shore. The water was quiet here, but Bill knew the current would get it. He began to strip off his clothing.

In about one minute the raft was whirling about in the swift current. It was hurled against large rocks in midstream, and the boys were thrown into the rough water.

Bill jumped into the river and swam toward the rocks. He saw a boy clinging to one.

"Hold on!" he called. "I'm coming!"

He was a good swimmer and very strong, but it was hard for him to fight that swift current. Finally he reached the rocks. The boy was his friend, Little Wren.

"Put your arm through mine and don't let go. Swim with your other arm. Use your legs. We'll get to shore."

It was hard work, but they made it. The other three were already on the shore. They were larger and stronger than Little Wren, but they were tired out from their struggle.

"You saved me, Bill!" cried Little Wren. "You were so brave. You risked your life."

The other boys crowded about Bill. They touched his hands, his arms, his hair. And all of them tried to thank him. They used English words, Sioux words, and sign language. But it all meant the same thing—Bill Cody was a brave boy, and they liked him.

Chief Rain-in-the-Face thanked Bill earnestly later on. "You saved my son. I'll never forget you."

BILL IS SEIZED AND TIED

One dark night around nine o'clock Bill Cody was on guard at the fort storehouse. This building was off by itself, between the stables and the river.

Suddenly he heard a noise in the direction of the stables. "Some horse is getting nervous," he thought. Presently he heard the same noise nearer. This wasn't a horse—he didn't know just what it was.

146

There were so many noises, the rushing river, rustling leaves, animals—there it was again, close by!

Bill lifted his gun to give the alarm, but he didn't have a chance to shoot. It was knocked out of his hands. He was seized and held. His mouth was stuffed with cloth. He couldn't make a sound, but he saw several shadowy forms.

Then he was tied to a heavy bench by the door. And all this time not a single word was spoken. Not a single face had he seen. But he was sure the men were Indians.

He heard them pry the door open. He saw shadowy figures enter the storehouse. Other shadowy figures appeared with pack mules. Supplies were brought out and loaded. Then the mules were led away.

Now he heard soft footsteps coming toward the bench. He heard a whisper. Then he closed his eyes and waited for the tomahawk to fall.

He was terrified. He thought of his mother and sisters. He would never see them again.

Silence now, silence so thick he could feel it. Why were they waiting? Five minutes passed—ten minutes——

Then he heard the next guard calling him. "Bill! Bill! Where are you?"

Now Matt lighted the lantern he always carried and looked about. He discovered Bill at once and cut the ropes. Then he took the gag from the boy's mouth.

In another minute he was firing his gun. In

only another minute or so officers and soldiers came running.

Of course it was Indians, they all said. They would pursue them tomorrow at daybreak, right to their camp village. The army would get back its supplies—no fear of that.

Now Captain Gray of Company C came running. He was hatless, coatless, and breathless.

"Colonel," he said as he saluted, "there isn't a man in C barracks! My whole troop has deserted!"

"Did the sentries posted tonight belong to your troop?"

"They did. Where are they?"

"I suppose they are on their way to California with our supplies."

"Oh!" cried Bill. "The men who stole the supplies weren't Indians?"

"Not one," answered the colonel grimly. "They were our own men. We will pursue them, of course," he said to the officers. "Be ready to start at dawn."

"I hope to be one of the party," said Captain Gray.

He was, and when he came back, he reported bad news. The deserters had been attacked by Indians and every man had been killed. A friendly Indian had told him this.

The Colonel sent to Fort Leavenworth at once for additional troops. Two of the young scouts carried the message by horseback.

No one blamed Bill Cody, but he blamed himself. "It's my fault," he told Mr. Carson. "I should have fired my gun the minute I heard that first noise."

"Noises out here are different, Bill. I could write a whole book about them. Would you like to have a few lessons?"

"Yes indeed! I'd be very thankful to you, Mr. Carson."

When Lew Simpson came back he found a very busy young guard. Lessons with Kit Carson on noises. Lessons with the Sioux boys on tracking. Lessons with soldiers on shooting. Lessons with cavalrymen on riding.

"I've learned a lot of things out here," Bill told Mr. Simpson as they started back east.

"I'm glad you have. You may need this knowledge some day."

"You mean if there's an Indian war?"

"I do. If there is, you'll be in it, Bill."

Trapping
Adventure

BILL reached the valley safely. He was glad to be home again and glad to see his folks, but he hadn't forgotten that shot from the Smith cabin.

"You needn't have gone," said Martha. "That wasn't Abel Smith who called at you."

"It was our farm hand," laughed Julia. "He just wanted to scare you."

"Well, he did—all the way to Wyoming!"

"Now you can go to school again," said his mother. "Mr. Woods wants you to come back."

But Bill had other plans. He was going into business with his friend Dave Harrington. They would go west and hunt beaver.

"He's a fine young man, but he's only eighteen," objected Mrs. Cody. "You two boys can't go off into the wilderness alone."

"Dave has hunted beaver ever since he was fourteen. And anyway we've already bought our outfit. We have a wagon, an ox team, and supplies. Dave is waiting for me now in Leavenworth."

"Then I shall say no more."

"Here is the rest of my pay, Ma. I've kept out all I need."

"You're a good son, Bill. I do hope you and Dave will have good luck."

"We will. I'm always lucky. Lew Simpson said I was born lucky."

It really seemed so. The boys had no trouble on their long journey to beaver land. So Dave had time to answer many questions Bill asked when they reached new country.

How far was this trail from the regular wag-

on routes to California? How far from the route to Fort Laramie? How far from the fort in Utah? How far from the Santa Fe Trail?

Fortunately Dave knew the answers, so now Bill had another teacher and new lessons every day. Mrs. Cody had no reason to worry. Her son was learning the very things he would need to know.

They had now reached the end of their journey, a lake high up in the hills. They built a dugout in a hillside with a small fireplace in one corner. They made two bunks, two small benches, and a table. Then they moved in their supplies and were cozy and comfortable.

Next a pen was made for the oxen. This was close to the dugout for safety. No wild animal would dare attack their team now.

They were lucky from the day they started to hunt. They found beaver, mink, and otter—so many more than they expected. Soon they had bundles of skins. They could go back now. They needn't wait till spring. They could start before the winter snows began.

But the night before they planned to leave a dreadful thing happened. A bear killed one of their oxen.

They heard the noise and rushed out with their guns. The bear leaped at Dave, and Bill fired. His aim was accurate. The bear was shot through the heart.

Now what would they do? One ox couldn't pull the wagon and a heavy load of furs. They must go to a settlement and buy another ox.

The nearest settlement was one hundred and twenty-five miles away! But there was nothing else they could do. They would drive their ox and take turns riding it.

However, the next morning another dreadful thing happened. Bill slipped on a wet stone and fell. His right leg was broken. Dave had to carry him to the dugout and set the broken bone the best he could, but he knew it wouldn't do. Bill needed a doctor, and there was none nearer than Leavenworth. This meant an ox team first. Dave must start at once for the settlement.

Bill tried to talk him out of it. Dave paid no attention. He went right on with preparations for his trip. These were all for Bill, however.

Fortunately Bill's bunk was close to the fireplace. He put food and water near by. The long-handled frying pan and a pile of wood were placed close by also. The candle, matches, and a book were on the table just back of his bed. A pile of beaver skins was on the floor. It might turn cold, and Bill could use them for covers.

Then Dave left, and young Bill Cody was all alone in that far-off wilderness.

WORSE AND WORSE

It would be at least twenty days before Dave could get back. To keep track of the time Bill cut a notch in a stick every day.

He cooked from his bunk. He threw wood in the fireplace from his bunk. He ate in bed. But the days seemed longer and longer.

At last he tried to read Dave's book. It was a reader, and he could understand a few lines. He was delighted and kept trying. When he could read a whole page, he was so happy he wanted to tell someone.

Maybe he could tell Dave today. He should come. It was the twentieth day. So, when he heard a loud noise outside the dugout, he thought it was his friend.

"Come in! Come in!" he cried joyfully.

The door was pushed open slowly. "This is strange," Bill thought. "Dave must be sick——"

"Dave!" he cried. "Dave! What is the matter with you?"

Now an Indian warrior entered. Others followed, and all were painted for war. Bill was

terrified. He knew what painted faces meant. He knew the Indians meant to kill him. He could tell by their actions.

One warrior came to his bed. It was Chief Rain-in-the-Face! He didn't seem to know Bill. He glared at him coldly.

"Don't you remember me?" the boy asked. "I'm Bill Cody. I'm Little Wren's friend."

The chief still glared at him. Bill remembered what Kit Carson had said, "Your friends will become your enemies."

"I saved your boy from drowning," Bill went on. "Don't you remember that raft at Fort Laramie?"

The chief nodded slightly, and Bill pleaded with him again. "Little Wren loved me. He wouldn't let anyone kill me. Surely you will save me. You said you would never forget that I saved your son."

Now Rain-in-the-Face grunted. He turned

away from the bed and talked with his warriors. Bill could see he was trying to persuade them. He was having a hard time, too. Some were shaking their heads.

After a while the chief told the boy they would spare his life. But they would take his gun and ammunition and food.

Bill pleaded with him. He said he was sick. He had a broken leg. How could he defend himself without his gun? How could he live without food?

"This is war," said the Indian. "And you are the enemy. The white men have robbed the Indians. Now we're taking what is yours."

And that was what they did. They took even his matches. The only food they left was a frozen deer carcass hanging on the wall.

He had to stay awake nearly all night now to keep his fire going. If it went out he would freeze to death. His only food was deer meat roasted over the blaze.

Then came a blizzard. Snow drifted into the room. It was so deep outside that the one window was covered. This was bad—it would keep Dave back. It proved to be bad for another reason. It brought hungry wolves to the dugout.

They had smelled the deer meat and were determined to get in. They began to scratch at the door, and Bill was frightened. He prayed they wouldn't be smart enough to push it. The door wasn't strong.

Then, while the wolves howled outside, William Frederick Cody made some promises to himself. If he got out of this alive, he would never leave a settlement again. He would go to school, too.

He did some deep thinking about other things. His mother had been right. Two boys had no business out in the wilderness alone.

You couldn't count on luck, either. There was no such thing as being born lucky. Just see what trouble he was in now! Would that flimsy door hold?

WOULDN'T DAVE EVER COME?

The twenty-fifth day! What had happened to Dave? The storm wouldn't delay him this long. He must have been killed by Indians. Then Bill broke down and cried.

"This won't do," he thought. "I mustn't lose my courage. Dave is all right. He'll come back. I know he'll come back."

Then he tried to think of something funny. Nothing seemed funny now. Oh, yes, the song Horace and his friends sang to the Indian trappers. Maybe he could sing it. He still remembered the tune.

> Ho, pretty beaver!
> Don't flap your tail at me!
> I came out west to find you.
> I want you on my knee.

163

Bill made up another stanza and sang it.

> Ho, pretty beaver!
> Don't wink your eye so bright!
> For sure as sin
> I'll have your skin
> Some cold and frosty night.

He thought he would make up another verse the next day, but he was too miserable. He couldn't even think of words that rhymed.

After this he didn't even try, he was too unhappy. His food wouldn't last much longer. Neither would his fire.

The twenty-ninth day! Bill threw his last stick of wood on the fire. He ate his last slice of meat. Now the room began to get cold. And more and more wolves came. He could tell by the frightful howls.

Around noon there was a rifleshot. Then another and another from close by. Had the warriors come back? Were they chasing the wolves away so they could come in?

He trembled in his bed. Then suddenly his misery was over. "Bill! Bill! I'm here!" It was Dave's voice.

In another minute Dave was in the cabin. And the sick boy wept again, but this time with joy.

Yes, Dave had been lost. He couldn't find the trail in the blizzard. But he was here, and he had brought another ox. He had supplies, too. Had Bill's food lasted?

When he heard Bill's story he said they would leave at once. But first Bill was to have a good dinner—fried rabbit, corn-meal cakes, and molasses.

Bill was to have a bath and clean clothing. Dave had brought clothes, new sheets, and a pillowcase from the settlement.

There were no more tears now. The little room was filled with warmth and talk and happy laughter.

That afternoon, after the furs had been loaded, Dave made a bed in the wagon. He carried Bill out and laid him on it carefully.

Oh, such a wonderful bed! Bill sighed with happiness as he sank down into the pile of soft beaver skins. He drew the lovely mink cover over him and sighed again.

"Ready?" called Dave from the driver's seat.

"Ready," answered the invalid.

Dave cracked his long whip. At once the oxen started.

"Eastbound for Leavenworth!" called the driver.

"Eastbound for Leavenworth!" called the passenger.

But what he thought was "Eastbound for home and Mother."

The Pony Express

A LARGE crowd gathered at the railroad station at St. Joseph, Missouri, April 3, 1860. They were waiting for the train from the East.

A wonderful thing was about to happen. From here, the mail would be carried to the Far West by Pony Express riders. It could go no farther by train. This was the end of the tracks.

"It can't be done," said a man in the crowd. "There are two thousand miles of plains, deserts, and mountains."

"But each rider only makes five stations," argued another man. "And the stations are only fifteen miles apart all the way."

"That's quite a trip if Indians are after you shooting arrows."

"And they will be," declared a trapper. "All the Plains tribes are angry about this Pony Express."

"Why?" asked a joker. "Do they want us to use smoke signals, too?"

The crowd laughed. Then a fur trader spoke seriously. "I can tell you why they are angry. They don't want iron tracks across their grazing land. Nor iron horses rushing over mountains and plains, scaring the game away."

"Nor do they want schoolhouses and colleges," said Mr. Ralph Woods, the teacher. "Indians must change their ideas."

"Well, they haven't changed their ideas yet," said the fur trader. "The Indians will make it hot for those Pony Express riders. I'd hate to be one of them."

"So would I," nodded the trapper.

"I understand the firm of Russell, Majors, and Waddell has charge of this express," said a lawyer in the crowd.

"It has," replied the trader. "The company has built every station and stocked each one with ponies."

Young Bill Cody stood close to the tracks. He watched a young rider pull up nearby. The rider jumped from his pony and stood by its side.

"He's one of the express riders," said a blacksmith. "I know him."

"A rider! That boy!" exclaimed his wife.

"He's sixteen, and he understands horses. He won't ride them to death the first hour."

"But he's too young," said an eastern woman.

Bill smiled to himself. He was only fourteen, but he was nearly as big as the Pony Express rider.

"A boy that age is a man out here on the frontier," said a hunter. "You don't need to worry about that young man. He grew up on the trails to the Far West."

Again Bill smiled to himself. Why, he grew up on those trails, too. Hadn't he been in the wilderness alone many times? And he was a good horseman. Everyone said he rode better than most men.

The woman from the East was now talking again. "When did that rider go to school?"

"School!" exclaimed the hunter. "Did you say school, Ma'am?"

The crowd laughed. Frontier boys didn't have schools to go to, nor the chance to go if one was started. They had to work.

"I don't see how he can deliver mail if he can't read or write."

"Ma'am, these riders must know a lot more than how to read and write. They are carefully chosen. They must be lightweight but strong."

"And excellent riders," added the blacksmith.

171

"They need to be crack shots, too," the trader said.

"But——" the lady began.

"You might say that a Pony Express rider has gone to schools all his life—the mountains, plains, and deserts have been his schools. His teachers have been trappers, scouts, wagon masters, and even Indians."

Just then Mr. Russell of Russell, Majors, and Waddell crossed to the Pony Express rider. Bill and the rest of the crowd moved closer so they could hear what was said.

"Am I in the right place, Mr. Russell?" the rider asked.

"Yes, the mail car stops here. Now listen, Jack, there are likely to be valuables in the mail sack, gold or money, or both. You must watch out for bandits."

"I'll watch, but they can't catch me—not if all your horses are as good as this one."

"They are, every one of them. They are all mustangs and fast runners."

"My goodness!" cried a woman who had overheard this. "My goodness! Mr. Russell said something about bandits!"

"Of course," nodded the trader. "Bandits have been holding up stagecoaches and taking the mailbags. Now they'll plan to hold up the Pony Express."

"Here comes the train!" shouted Bill.

The crowd watched closely now. People didn't want to miss one thing that happened. This day, April 3, 1860, would be one of the great days in history. Everyone would tell his children and grandchildren about it in years to come.

The train stopped. A leather mailbag was handed to Mr. Russell. It was locked and sealed. Now it was slung across the rider's shoulder, and the key was given to him.

Jack jumped on his pony and was off in a flash.

The crowd cheered. The train whistle blew. Bells rang. The Pony Express had started. Hooray! Hooray!

"Mr. Russell," Bill Cody called above the noise. "Mr. Russell, I'd like to be one of your riders."

The big man worked his way through the cheering crowd to Bill's side. "I don't know, Bill, I——"

The eager boy interrupted him. "I'm as big as the rider who just left here, and I'm strong. I can handle horses and shoot. Mr. Majors told me I could always have a job with your company."

"Easy, Bill. Slow up! We do need experienced riders, but I'll have to think about it. The only openings we have now are farther west of here—it's dangerous country."

"I'm not afraid, Mr. Russell. I've faced danger before. Please give me a chance."

"We'll see, Bill. We'll see."

THE MAIL MUST GO THROUGH!

Bill Cody got his chance. On his first trip, nothing happened. He made his seventy-five miles in the scheduled time.

Then came trouble, plenty of trouble. Arrows whizzed past him. Bullets sang around him, but he escaped every time.

One day some fifteen Indians crowded him into a ravine and shot at him. The young rider flattened out on his pony and rode like the wind. He was soon out of danger. The Indians couldn't keep up with him.

Once he was held up by bandits who took his mail pouch and rode away. But Bill had fooled them. They had taken an empty bag filled with paper. The mail pouch was hidden under Bill's saddlebags.

Other riders weren't so lucky. Some had been killed. One time Bill rode an extra three stations for one of these men. It was an extra forty-five miles for a young boy who had already ridden seventy-five miles. But he did it—many times. He was used to long hours in the saddle.

Another time Bill rode over three hundred miles without sleep. He stopped only to change horses, and he used twenty-one different steeds. This ride set a Pony Express record that was never broken. *The mail must go through!*

Now the Indians had a new trick. They drove off the extra horses at every station. The Pony Express was helpless. It had to be stopped for several weeks.

The riders didn't have a vacation, however. They formed a band to pursue the Indians and recover the horses. Others joined them—stock tenders, hunters, traders, trappers, and ranch-men. They agreed that these Indians had to be taught one thing—*the mail must go through.*

They agreed also that Bill Cody couldn't go with them. They were going on a dangerous trip into Indian country. And Bill was too young for this kind of work. He might do something foolish just to show off. He might even ruin their expedition.

Bill was disappointed. It was a slap in the face. If he was smart enough to be a rider, he was certainly smart enough to go on a horse hunt.

Finally he went to the leader. In just five minutes this gentleman found out what Mrs. Cody had known for a long time—that Bill was a good talker.

"Well, Bill, you've talked me into it. You may go with us.

These men watched Bill from the time they

left the station. They watched the way he treated his horse. They watched all his actions.

"There's nothing foolish about that boy," they told one another. "He's quiet and doesn't try to show off."

The party had now reached Indian country and moved with caution. Their scouts reported that horses with shoes had come this way.

The same afternoon scouts discovered a large herd of horses grazing near an Indian camp. It was a large camp, but there were no women and children.

The white men made their plans. They hadn't come to kill Indians. They wanted only to frighten them and get the horses. So they would wait till dark, creep up on the camp, and surprise the braves.

At dark the leader gave the signal. The men crept up quietly. When they reached the camp, they rode through it yelling and firing into the air. They circled the camp and rode through again yelling and firing.

The surprised braves fled in all directions. The white men rounded up the stolen horses and went back to the station.

In a week's time the Pony Express was running again, and Bill Cody was one of its favorite riders. All the men liked him.

"He'll go out of his way to do a fellow a favor," said a stock tender.

"He's certainly the luckiest rider on the road," said another rider. "He always gets out of trouble some way."

"I never saw the likes of him," said a station manager. "He'll gallop in here with a bullet hole in his hat and never mention it. He's not even nervous when he's changing his saddle."

All this talk didn't deceive Bill. He knew why he was lucky. He was always watching for danger. He was never off guard.

Besides, he had keen eyes and a quick trigger finger. His aim was always accurate.

"We didn't make a mistake when we hired young Bill Cody," Mr. Majors told his partners.

"Indeed we didn't," replied Mr. Russell. "He'll get the mail through if he lives. Neither arrows nor bullets, nor rain nor snow, nor cold nor heat, can keep that young rider from doing his duty."

Buffalo Bill

IN THE spring of 1883 a newspaper reporter called on the western manager of the Kansas Pacific Railroad. He said his paper, the *Omaha Bee,* would like to know about the work Colonel William Cody had done for that railroad some time before.

"That was a long time ago," said the manager, "when he was quite young. But we have the records—you can see for yourself."

The reporter looked and whistled. "Why, this shows he killed some four thousand buffaloes in about eighteen months!"

"That's correct. We had twelve hundred

hands laying tracks, and Cody kept them supplied with buffalo meat. It was very dangerous work. He was likely to be shot any time by hostile Indians."

"Did he have any trouble with them?"

"Plenty. The Indians were determined to stop the building of the railroad. They killed so many workmen we had to get soldiers to protect them."

"It's a wonder they didn't protect Cody."

"They did finally. We wouldn't let him risk his life. And that's what he did every time he went after buffalo."

"Did he follow the herd and shoot an animal from behind?"

"Not he! He would ride into a big herd and gallop along by the beast he wanted. Then he shot down at its heart."

"That took courage."

"Great courage. We paid him five hundred dollars a month, and he was worth it."

183

"No wonder he was called Buffalo Bill."

"Our men thought he deserved that name. They wanted to honor him in some way. Cody was proud of the name then."

"He still is. He said so recently."

"Young man, tell your paper that Bill Cody did a great service for the United States. With his help we were able to lay the tracks across the plains."

"And he was only twenty-one at the time!"

"That's all. Now why do you want this information?"

"Mr. Cody is bringing his Wild West Show to Omaha in May. The papers will print a good deal about him. They want every detail we can get."

"It's a great show. Bill told me all about it. He wants Eastern people to see what the West was like some twenty years ago."

"He's bringing real Indians, cowboys, coach

184

drivers, Pony Express riders, scouts, plainsmen, and sharpshooters. At least, that's what he's advertising.

"He'll have them. There will be plenty of good riding and good shooting. I hope it will be a grand success. Bill deserves it. No man knows the West better. No man has risked his life more to settle it."

CHIEF OF SCOUTS FOR THE FIFTH U.S. CAVALRY

A newspaper reporter was admitted to the office of General Phil Sheridan in Washington, D.C., in 1884. He said his paper, the *New York Times*, would like certain information regarding William Cody as an army scout.

"You see, General, Mr. Cody's Wild West Show is in New York now. It is drawing immense crowds. Some go to see the Indians, but I think most go to see Mr. Cody himself."

The general nodded. "I went, and I was delighted. Mr. Cody made a wonderful picture when he led the parade riding his great white horse. The people went wild."

"They went wild when they saw him shoot, too. He's the finest marksman New York has ever seen. People want to know all about him."

"I can tell you about his scouting. This happened in 1870 when our army had been sent west to settle the Indians for good. Mr. Cody guided us at times, and I found I could always trust his judgment. He would carry messages through the most dangerous Indian country. He would start out in the black of night, when other scouts had refused to go.

"He had endless courage. His services were so valuable I made him chief of scouts for the Fifth Cavalry.

"His pay? Well, he was a civilian scout, but he received as much pay as a colonel."

"Oh! Then he wasn't a colonel?"

"No, he didn't belong to our forces, except when he was serving as a scout. People called him Colonel later on just to honor him."

"When did he begin to wear long hair?"

The general smiled. "When he was with the army. All the scouts had long hair. It was the fashion. And Bill had to be a dandy like the others."

"Thank you, General Sheridan. Your words will be read by thousands of people in New York tomorrow."

"I hope they will all go to Bill's show."

"I hope so, too, General!"

A month later, a reporter from the *Boston Herald* called on General E. A. Carr in Washington, D.C. His paper wanted information regarding William Frederick Cody, he said.

Cody's Wild West Show was in Boston now and was playing to big crowds. It was the best

open-air show ever seen there. No side shows, no clowns, no fat ladies, no fakes of any kind. There were only pure western acts, and each one was a sensation.

"I'm very glad," said the general. "I was very fond of Bill. He knew those plains as well as I know my own back yard. He could guide us wherever our troops had to go."

"Did he get along with the officers?"

"They treated him as one of them. He was very modest and never boasted about his work. He was always a gentleman. He was never rough or quarrelsome."

"Was he a good scout?"

"The best I ever saw. His eyesight was better than a good field glass. He was a perfect judge of distance. He could tell correctly the number of miles to water. We always knew how to use our canteens when he guided us."

"How about trailing Indians?"

"He was wonderful. He would see signs no one else could see. It was the same way when he was looking for stray animals or game. He was a marvelous hunter."

"Thank you, General Carr. Your words will be in the *Herald* tomorrow."

CODY'S WILD WEST SHOW IN LONDON

The English had never seen an outdoor show like this. Real Indians, real cowboys, real plainsmen. There was even an old stagecoach which the Indians attacked in a make-believe fight. Its make-believe passengers were rescued by yelling, galloping cowboys.

Everyone in London wanted to see the show. Queen Victoria saw it twice. The second time she had some three hundred guests with her. All of them were kings, queens, princes, or dukes, with their wives or husbands and children.

Queen Victoria sent for Mr. Cody and thanked him for the splendid performance. And Mr. Cody was as gracious and courteous as any of the dukes and princes.

"Colonel Cody," the queen said, "you have made us understand America better."

After the English season was over, Mr. Cody sailed home on the "Persian Monarch" as a hero. When he arrived, there was a great crowd at the harbor to greet him.

He stood on the captain's bridge. The people saw his tall and striking figure and his long hair waving in the breeze.

"Oh! There he is! Isn't he handsome!"

A hundred persons said this, and a hundred more declared he was the handsomest man they had ever seen.

People paid more attention to Mr. Cody than they did to the gaily dressed Indians leaning over the ship's rail.

General Sherman wrote Colonel Cody at once and congratulated him. He said, "You have shown an important phase in our country's history. Without this, the plains would still be too dangerous to cross.

"You have played a great part in the real events, Bill. Keep on playing your role in the picture."